Samuel French Acting Edition

I0591570

The Healing

by Samuel D. Hunter

SAMUELFRENCH.COM   SAMUELFRENCH.CO.UK

FOR PRODUCTION ENQUIRIES
UNITED STATES AND CANADA
Info@SamuelFrench.com
1-866-598-8449

UNITED KINGDOM AND EUROPE
Plays@SamuelFrench.co.uk
020-7255-4302

Each title is subject to availability from Samuel French, depending
upon country of performance. Please be aware that *THE HEALING* may
not be licensed by Samuel French in your territory. Professional and
amateur producers should contact the nearest Samuel French office or
licensing partner to verify availability.

MUSIC USE NOTE

Licensees are solely responsible for obtaining formal written permission from copyright owners to use copyrighted music in the performance of this play and are strongly cautioned to do so. If no such permission is obtained by the licensee, then the licensee must use only original music that the licensee owns and controls. Licensees are solely responsible and liable for all music clearances and shall indemnify the copyright owners of the play(s) and their licensing agent, Samuel French, against any costs, expenses, losses and liabilities arising from the use of music by licensees. Please contact the appropriate music licensing authority in your territory for the rights to any incidental music.

IMPORTANT BILLING AND CREDIT REQUIREMENTS

If you have obtained performance rights to this title, please refer to your licensing agreement for important billing and credit requirements.

THE HEALING was commissioned and first produced Off Broadway by Theater Breaking Through Barriers (Nicholas Viselli, Producing Artistic Director; Steve Asher, General Manager) on June 22, 2016. The production was directed by Stella Powell-Jones, with dramaturgy by John M. Baker, sets by Jason Simms, costumes by Christopher Metzger, lighting by Alejandro Fajardo, sound by Brandon Wolcott, and props by Charles Bowden. The Production Stage Manager was Anne Huston, and the Assistant Stage Manager was Seth Kieser. The cast was as follows:

SHARON	Shannon DeVido
DONALD	David Harrell
BONNIE	Jamie Petrone
GREG	John McGinty
LAURA	Mary Theresa Archbold
ZOE	Pamela Sabaugh
JOAN	Lynne Lipton
VOICE	Lynne McCollough

THE HEALING was developed, in part, through a residency at Space at Ryder Farm.

CHARACTERS

SHARON – Thirties, female. Played by an actress who uses a wheelchair.

DONALD – Thirties, male. Played by an actor with a disability.

BONNIE – Thirties, female. Played by an actress with a disability.

GREG – Thirties, male. Played by a deaf actor.

LAURA – Thirties, female. Played by an actress with a disability.

ZOE – Thirties, female. Played by an actress with a disability.

JOAN – Sixties, female. Played by an actress without a disability.

A VOICE – Male or female, the voice of a shopping channel on the TV.

SETTING

The main room of a small, unimpressive house in a small town in southeastern Idaho, near Idaho Falls.

A couch is in the space, as well as a small TV. Covering almost every surface in the house are small keepsakes and trinkets: cheaply made little statues (of frogs, chiefly), decorations, keepsakes, holiday decorations, etc.

Scattered around the floor are several boxes with packing materials, tape, etc.

A hallway offstage leads to the bedroom and bathroom, a kitchen offstage.

TIME

The present.

AUTHOR'S NOTES

Dialogue written in *italics* is emphatic, deliberate; dialogue in ALL CAPS is impulsive, explosive.

A slash (/) indicates an overlap in dialogue. Whenever a slash appears, the following line of dialogue should begin.

Ellipses (…) indicate when a character is trailing off, dashes (–) indicate where a character is being cut off, either by another character or themself.

For Greg: dialogue that is <u>underlined</u> indicates when he is signing and it is not being translated, dialogue that is **bold** indicates when he is signing and Bonnie is translating. Dialogue that is signed and voiced simultaneously is designated as "simcom." All other dialogue is voiced. Bonnie interprets for Greg as appropriate.

(As the lights go to black, a **VOICE** *fills the theater, mid-sentence:)*

VOICE. – and it's really such a great deal, here if you can see this here – three easy payments of just $19.99 plus shipping. And really this is a keepsake that will last a lifetime, *more* than a lifetime, this is something that can be passed down in your family from generation to generation, you know – it's really just going to become an heirloom, a family heirloom. So, yeah – I'd just get on that right now. And next up we have this lovely –

(The **VOICE** *is suddenly cut off and lights snap on, revealing:)*

(Early evening.)

*(***DONALD** *and* **SHARON** *sit together, both dressed in funeral black. They are both eating cake off of paper plates, watching the TV, which faces upstage. The* **VOICE** *is now playing at a low level on the TV; loud enough that we know it's there, but not loud enough to be understandable.)*

(They watch and eat. Finally:)

DONALD. Who was –…?

(Pause.)

SHARON. Hm?

DONALD. The lady with the red suit, the red pants suit.

SHARON. Oh, that's –…

(Pause.)

I don't know.

(Pause.)

DONALD. Red pants suit, what the hell?

(Silence. **SHARON** *and* **DONALD** *continue to eat, watch TV.)*

(Finally:)

SHARON. She fuckin' called me "Sherry."

*(***DONALD*** *snorts.)*

DONALD. *Who was that?!*

SHARON. I don't know.

DONALD. Has anyone ever called you that?

SHARON. Not until today.

DONALD. Who wears a red pants suit to a *funeral?*

(Silence. They eat and watch TV.)

You know when I saw her in the coffin, I was thinking / like –

SHARON. Casket.

DONALD. What?

SHARON. It's a casket, not a coffin.

*(***DONALD*** *glares at her.)*

Seriously, I've spent the last three days dealing with all this funeral crap, I know the difference / between –

DONALD. *Anyway* when I saw her in there, for the first time I was like – wait, she had a bump on her nose?

SHARON. What do you mean?

DONALD. Like – I didn't realize Zoe had a little bump on her nose. Until I saw her in the coffin. Casket.

(Pause.)

SHARON. Wait how did you not know that?

DONALD. I don't know, I just never –… I never *stared* at her nose.

(Pause.)

You knew she –?

SHARON. Yeah.

DONALD. So if two months ago I had casually referred to the bump on her nose, you would have been like, "Oh right."

SHARON. Yes, though I'm having trouble imagining what conversation / would have –

DONALD. *Really?!*

SHARON. *Yes.*

(*Pause.*)

DONALD. Huh.

(*Pause.*)

It just made me think, like – what else did I miss? There's probably a lot else that I missed. Like – what was her favorite movie? I have *no idea* what her favorite movie was.

SHARON. This cake is making me sick.

DONALD. Stop eating it.

SHARON. No it's *so good.*

(*Pause. They continue to watch and eat.*)

DONALD. Do you think we could have – done something?

SHARON. No, she –. No.

(*Pause.*)

DONALD. I didn't know things had gotten this bad for her, if I knew that / she –

SHARON. There's nothing we could have done.

DONALD. I know, I just –

SHARON. There's nothing we could have done. Stop.

(*Silence. They watch the TV.*)

DONALD. Why are we watching the shopping channel?

SHARON. I can't find the remote, it might be gone. I don't think Zoe ever watched anything else.

(*Pause. They watch.*)

DONALD. What is that?

SHARON. The –? What they're selling? It's a –… I don't know what it is. Christmas ornament? No.

DONALD. I don't know if we're gonna be able to pack up this place by Tuesday.

SHARON. I know. There's tons of stuff in the second bedroom, too. There's this clown figurine holding an umbrella that just makes me angry for some reason.

(Silence. They eat. The TV plays.)

(Suddenly:)

DONALD. This is terrible to ask and I hate myself for even thinking it, but do you think I could take the riding lawn mower?

SHARON. That's not terrible.

DONALD. Really?

SHARON. No, you're fine. I'm taking the juicer.

DONALD. I just –. I don't know, I thought she wouldn't mind.

SHARON. She wouldn't, just take it. But how are you gonna get it to Boise?

DONALD. Oh. Right. I mean I could –… No, that's stupid.

(Pause.)

How much did you have to pay for the funeral?

SHARON. Don't worry about it.

DONALD. Zoe didn't have any money in her bank account, or –?

SHARON. Some. Not enough.

(Short pause.)

DONALD. I'll chip in, but I'm gonna have to wait for a month / or two –

SHARON. Don't worry about it.

DONALD. They cut my hours *again*, and anyway I –…

(Short pause.)

I'll get you some money.

SHARON. It's okay. Work's been good lately, it's fine.

(Pause. They watch TV.)

DONALD. I didn't realize that she didn't really have – *any* family left.

SHARON. Her uncle was there, the guy from Montana? Anyway I hope he was her uncle, he's taking her ashes, so.

DONALD. He was on something, right?

SHARON. Yes he most certainly was.

DONALD. But yeah, I figured she had *someone*. Cousins, or –. It never really occurred to me that someone could have no family.

SHARON. Yeah I hate that she didn't have anyone here in town.

DONALD. I mean she had Joan.

*(**SHARON** bristles. Pause. **DONALD** looks at her.)*

You're still mad at me.

SHARON. No –

DONALD. Yes you are, you're totally still mad at me –

SHARON. Please, I'm tired, I / don't –

DONALD. She would have shown up anyway, it's a small town –

SHARON. Well you didn't need to *invite* her to the funeral, Donald.

DONALD. I didn't *invite her*, it was just a *courtesy call* to let her know when it was happening –

*(**SHARON**'s phone rings. She takes it out of her pocket.)*

I'm sorry I invited Joan to the funeral, okay? I was just trying to do / the right thing.

SHARON. *(Answering her phone.)* Hey, Marsha. Could you actually give me like another hour or two before you pick me up? Is that cool?

> (**SHARON** *listens.* **DONALD** *starts moving around the space, looking at all the trinkets.*)

Oh.

> *(Listens.)*

Shit. Well, yeah, I –...

> *(Listens.)*

No, it's okay, I understand. Yeah, totally. I'm sure I can find someone. Do you need me to change your flight, or –?

DONALD. What's going on?

> (**SHARON** *waves* **DONALD** *away, listening.*)

SHARON. Really, Marsha, it's okay. I'll see you later. Bye.

> (**SHARON** *hangs up.*)

Shit.

DONALD. What?

SHARON. It's – nothing. My aide has to fly back to Chicago tonight.

DONALD. Why?

SHARON. Her cat sitter's mother died.

DONALD. Were they – close?

SHARON. No, it's not that, it's –. Her cat sitter has to go to Milwaukee so no one is there to take care of her stupid cat, so.

DONALD. Oh.

SHARON. It's okay, I can find someone. I've got a couple people in Denver I use when I'm there, I can probably get someone on a flight to Boise tonight.

DONALD. Sharon if you need someone to help you out, I can –

SHARON. It's fine.

(SHARON scrolls through her phone. DONALD starts wrapping up some of the trinkets in bubble wrap and putting them in boxes.)

DONALD. I mean I've done it before, it's been a while but if you just direct me –

SHARON. It's fine, don't worry about it.

DONALD. You don't need to spend all that money –

SHARON. I have miles, it's fine, just –.

(SHARON dials.)

DONALD. Seriously, I don't mind, just tell me what to do and I'll do it. / It's not like I'm doing anything else.

SHARON. *(On the phone.)* Hey, Brendan. Listen – this is gonna sound sort of crazy but I'm out in Idaho right now, near that religious camp where I used to spend summers as a kid? Anyway turns out my regular aide has to fly back to Chicago tonight. Is there *any possible way* that you or maybe Cindy could come out for just a few days? Yeah, starting tonight. It's a little town called Rigby outside of Idaho Falls, I think I could –…

(SHARON listens. DONALD continues to pack.)

You're *sure?*

(Pause.)

No, I understand. Yeah. Okay, thanks, bye.

(SHARON hangs up.)

Shit.

DONALD. Sharon.

SHARON. It's okay, I know a few people in Austin, just let me send some texts –

DONALD. *Sharon.*

(SHARON looks at DONALD. Short pause.)

Just let me help?

(A doorbell.)

SHARON. *(Calling out.)* Door's open.

(BONNIE and GREG enter. BONNIE holds a store-bought meat and cheese tray.)

BONNIE. Hey there.

DONALD. Hey, Bonnie.

(DONALD goes to BONNIE, hugging her.)

BONNIE. *(Simcom.)* We're *so* sorry. Our flight, it –. We're just sorry for missing the funeral.

SHARON. We told you to come yesterday.

BONNIE. *(Simcom.)* I know but we just couldn't find any decent flights out of Spokane, we thought about driving but, you know, the highway this time of year, I was worried we'd get snowed in –

DONALD. It's okay.

BONNIE. Well, we're just –. Anyway, I still can't believe Zoe's gone, I'm in shock!

DONALD. Yeah, it's crazy.

BONNIE. It's just so tragic, it could happen to any of us!

DONALD. Yeah...

(Pause. DONALD and SHARON exchange a look.)

BONNIE. These freak accidents, it just –. I still can't wrap my head around it. I feel like she's gonna just walk right in through that door.

DONALD. Sure.

BONNIE. Just right now! Just walk right in, just now!

DONALD. Yeah, well, she –. Won't.

(Awkward pause. BONNIE looks at GREG.)

BONNIE. *(Simcom.)* Oh sorry! This is Greg.

GREG. Hi.

SHARON. / Hi.

DONALD. Hey.

BONNIE. *(Simcom.)* This is – Donald and Sharon.

(BONNIE spells out "Donald" and "Sharon" for GREG. It takes her a moment.)

(To DONALD *and* SHARON.*)* I'm still learning.

GREG. <u>You're doing fine!</u>

BONNIE. *(To* GREG, *simcom.)* We shared a bunk together with Zoe, every summer.

GREG. <u>They let you share a bunk with a boy?</u>

BONNIE. He's wondering why they let us share a bunk with a boy.

DONALD. Oh. Well, Joan didn't want me to at first, but she realized pretty quick I was just going to sneak in there anyway.

GREG. Ladies man!

DONALD. Yeah, more like a girly boy.

GREG. Oh.

> *(Pause.)*

I'm sorry.

DONALD. Thank – you?

> **(**BONNIE *looks around at all the trinkets in the room.)*

BONNIE. Wow, there are… There are – a lot more little thingies in here.

SHARON. Yeah, she just kept buying stuff, I guess.

BONNIE. Oh, we got this.

> **(**BONNIE *indicates the meat and cheese tray.)*

DONALD. We actually have a crazy amount of leftovers, maybe tomorrow we should try going to the food bank or something?

BONNIE. Sorry, I didn't think everyone would be gone already.

SHARON. It's almost seven.

BONNIE. I know what time it is, Sharon.

GREG. <u>Is there a bathroom?</u>

BONNIE. *(Simcom.)* Down the hall there, on the right.

> **(**GREG *exits.)*

What are we gonna do with all this stuff?

DONALD. Goodwill, most of it. I'm renting a U-haul tomorrow for the furniture. A lot of it will have to go in the trash –

SHARON. I have a system.

DONALD. Sharon has a system. How was the flight?

BONNIE. Awful. Took three hours to take off, then once we were in the air the woman beside me kept telling me how "inspiring" I was. I'm starving, can I –?

DONALD. Here, I'll make you a plate.

BONNIE. Oh, honey, you don't have to –

DONALD. It's fine, just relax.

>   (**DONALD** *goes into the kitchen.*)

>   (*An awkward silence between* **BONNIE** *and* **SHARON**.)

BONNIE. How – was it?

SHARON. Fine, I guess. It was at this depressing little funeral chapel in Idaho Falls, it was fine.

BONNIE. Well, it was really nice of you to organize it.

SHARON. There was barely anyone there.

BONNIE. Really? I figured that most of the people from her church would be there –

SHARON. They don't really do funerals, remember?

BONNIE. Oh, right.

>   (*Pause.*)

SHARON. Charlie Thompson was there.

BONNIE. *No.*

SHARON. Yep. And he *came up to me.*

BONNIE. Ew!

SHARON. I know! He did it in this disgusting way, too, he like came up to me and he was like – "I'm so, so sorry for your loss."

>   (*Pause.* **DONALD** *returns with a plate, hands it to* **BONNIE**.)

BONNIE. I mean that's not too weird?

SHARON. No it was like the way he said it.

DONALD. Are you still talking about Charlie Thompson?

SHARON. He was being gross.

DONALD. He was not, he was just / trying to –

SHARON. Are you *defending* him?

DONALD. I'm not, he's terrible, he's a loser and he's terrible, but I'm just saying – that one isolated interaction he had with you was *normal.*

SHARON. I can't believe you're defending him!

DONALD. I'm not –! I'm just saying, that taken out of context from the rest of his personality and the history of his life, that one isolated moment in time was not weird or disgusting.

SHARON. I'm sorry but when a twenty-five-year-old counselor makes a pass at a thirteen-year-old camper? That makes *everything* about him creepy. *Every moment of his life.*

DONALD. / Alright, alright.

BONNIE. Is this chicken or pork?

DONALD. Pork?

BONNIE. Ooo…

DONALD. You don't eat pork now?

BONNIE. I've read too many articles.

SHARON. Chicken's worse.

BONNIE. I don't wanna know, I like chicken.

SHARON. They think that like one in every three pieces of chicken is / tainted with salmonella and that's just like people *guessing* –

BONNIE. I don't wanna know I said!

SHARON. – seriously I could show you some videos / online, you wouldn't believe what –

DONALD. / Okay, okay, guys, c'mon –

BONNIE. *(Louder.)* I'm not listening I'm not listening I'm –

*(Suddenly, **LAURA** enters from the hall. She's wearing pajamas and has a sleeping mask around her neck.)*

(She stares at them for a moment. Silence.)

SHARON. Sorry.

*(**LAURA** stares at them. Another silence.)*

BONNIE. Hey, Laura.

LAURA. Hi.

*(Another pause. **LAURA** exits back into the bedroom.)*

BONNIE. *(Hushed.)* She's *sleeping* here?

SHARON. In Zoe's bed.

BONNIE. In *Zoe's bed*?!

DONALD. The second bedroom is full of crap, she couldn't sleep in there –

BONNIE. *That's still not okay.* We all got hotel rooms. And why is she in bed already?

SHARON. Migraine.

DONALD. *(To **BONNIE**.)* I think there's pasta salad, you want that instead?

BONNIE. Yes, please.

*(**DONALD** exits back into the kitchen with **BONNIE**'s plate. **BONNIE** looks at the TV.)*

Why are you watching the shopping channel?

SHARON. We can't find the remote.

BONNIE. You could just turn it off.

SHARON. Nah, it's too quiet in here.

BONNIE. Oh, and – you had to chip in for the funeral?

SHARON. Yeah, I did.

BONNIE. I'd love to help out – maybe next month?

(Pause.)

SHARON. Sure.

(Pause.)

BONNIE. How's Jim?

SHARON. Tim, Bonnie. His name is Tim.

BONNIE. Right sorry right.

SHARON. We split up.

BONNIE. Oh.

> *(Pause.)*

I'm – sorry?

SHARON. Nah.

BONNIE. Oh, good.

> *(Pause.)*

How's work?

SHARON. Uh – okay. The last couple years have been a little tough, but. Travel is expensive, and it's getting harder to make companies pay for accessible vans and aides to travel with, so whatever.

BONNIE. You travel often?

SHARON. Yeah, work in Chicago has pretty much dried up so I'm on the road a lot. Mostly to the same three or four cities. I've seen more of Tulsa than I ever wanted to, I'll say that much.

BONNIE. And it's –? Sorry, you make like – search engines?

SHARON. I mean I don't *make* them, it's –. It's metadata, it's like – I help to improve existing search engines on websites by creating searchable terms and –. Essentially I get hired by companies to make it easier for their customers to find stuff on their websites. That's basically it.

BONNIE. That's really great. I remember when you told me you wanted to become a librarian, I was like – uh oh!

> *(Pause.)*

SHARON. What?

BONNIE. I'm just saying, this is a lot better than being a librarian.

SHARON. I got my masters in library and information science, Bonnie.

BONNIE. I know.

SHARON. This is in my field, this is information science and / metadata –

BONNIE. I'm just saying it's good you're not a librarian! That's all I'm saying!

> (**DONALD** *comes out of the kitchen with a plate of food for* **BONNIE**. **BONNIE** *stops packing, takes the food.*)

DONALD. Anyone want wine?

BONNIE. Sure.

SHARON. I'm fine.

> (**GREG** *re-enters.*)

DONALD. Greg, you want some wine?

GREG. <u>Sure.</u>

> (**GREG** *follows* **DONALD** *into the kitchen.*)

BONNIE. But the funeral was nice?

DONALD. *(Offstage.)* Yeah, it was fine.

SHARON. It was weird.

DONALD. *(Offstage.)* It was *fine*. Zoe would have liked it, she would have enjoyed it.

SHARON. She would have enjoyed her own funeral?

> (**DONALD** *and* **GREG** *re-enter with wine and solo cups.* **DONALD** *pours wine for everyone.*)

DONALD. I'm just saying it was nice, *God*.

BONNIE. It's weird being this close to the camp. We drove past it on our way here, crazy to see it all abandoned like that. Zoe must've seen Joan in town every so often, that must have been weird.

GREG. <u>Who are you talking about?</u>

BONNIE. *(Simcom.)* I told you about her, she ran the camp.

GREG. <u>The religious lady?</u>

BONNIE. Yeah, the religious lady.

SHARON. Yeah, religious as in telling all of us that if we prayed hard enough Jesus would heal our broken little bodies.

GREG. **If she said stuff like that, why did people send their kids there?**

DONALD. I mean we were the only kids with disabilities at the camp, so I think we got it more than anyone else. And I don't think my parents really knew that Joan was a Christian Scientist, they just thought it was a Christian camp. They were pretty horrified years later when I told them about the stuff Joan said to us.

BONNIE. *(Simcom.)* Yeah, I mean, when Sharon got it shut down, our parents didn't / really –

SHARON. What do you mean I got it shut down? *We* got it shut down.

(**SHARON**'s *phone chimes. She looks at it.*)

BONNIE. Oh, I know, I just meant –. Whatever.

SHARON. *Shit.*

BONNIE. What?

SHARON. It's fine, it's –. I'm just having trouble getting an aide out here.

BONNIE. You don't have someone with you?

SHARON. She had to fly back to Chicago. But I've texted some people, I'll find someone.

BONNIE. One of us can help you out.

DONALD. That's what I said.

SHARON. / No, it's fine –

BONNIE. We've got an extra bed in our hotel room, just stay with us!

SHARON. Thank you, but I / can find someone, it's not –

DONALD. / Why is this such big deal?

BONNIE. Oh don't be silly, it's just a few nights –

SHARON. *It's really fine.*

> *(Pause.)*

Sorry, just –. It's fine.

> *(A silence. The TV plays.)*

DONALD. *(To* BONNIE.*)* So, how long have you and Greg been…?

BONNIE. *(Simcom.)* Oh, it's been eight months or so.

GREG. Nine, babe.

BONNIE. *(Simcom.)* Nine. This is our first trip together. Wish it could have been to Key Largo…

GREG. I *love* Key Largo.

BONNIE. Greg really loves Key Largo. He's from North Dakota, so.

> (BONNIE *reaches for her wine.* SHARON *and* DONALD *give each other a look.)*

> (GREG *gets up to refill his wine, browsing through some books on a bookshelf.)*

Donald, are you seeing anyone?

DONALD. Oh, no.

BONNIE. What about Rich?

DONALD. Rich from like three years ago? Oh, no, that wasn't anything. I actually sort of –… I mean this is going to sound weird, but I'm sort of – *okay* with not being with anyone right now?

SHARON. Yes, thank you!

DONALD. Yeah?

SHARON. I feel the exact same way, when I finally stopped telling myself over and over and over that I needed to be with someone, I was like – wow, this is nice. I'm gonna watch a movie and not feel terrible about myself.

> (GREG *pulls out a well-worn book, starts leafing through it.)*

DONALD. Right?! Once I finally just let go of the expectation, it was so liberating. I mean I'm not saying I'm gonna be single for the rest of my life –

SHARON. No, totally –

DONALD. But right now, I'm just – okay with it!

SHARON. Yes!

BONNIE. Well, I think you'll both find happiness someday. I know you will.

> *(Pause.)*

DONALD. Yeah, I –

> *(Deciding not to engage.)*

Yeah.

> **(SHARON** *sees the book that* **GREG** *is reading. She stops. Pause.)*

(To **SHARON.***)* What?

> **(SHARON** *moves toward* **GREG. DONALD** *and* **BONNIE** *see the book* **GREG** *is holding, they recognize it immediately.)*

SHARON. *(To* **GREG.***)* Can I see it?

> **(GREG** *looks at* **SHARON. SHARON** *takes the book from him. She opens it, leafing through it a bit.)*

(Reading.) "Mind must be found superior to all the beliefs of the five corporeal senses, and able to destroy all ills. Sickness is a belief, which must be annihilated by the divine Mind. Disease is an experience of the so-called mortal mind. It is fear made manifest on the body."

> **(SHARON** *flips through the book.* **GREG** *looks at* **BONNIE,** *confused.)*

DONALD. Sharon, c'mon –

SHARON. Highlights on almost every page.

> *(Pause. Finally,* **SHARON** *closes the book, addresses everyone.)*

I'm gonna do some more work in here and then get started on the kitchen.

> *(Pause.)*

DONALD. Sure. I'll start with the garage.

> (*To* GREG *and* BONNIE.)

If you guys are up for it, there's a ton of stuff to go through in the second bedroom?

BONNIE. Oh, sure.

> (BONNIE *and* GREG *begin to leave.*)

GREG. <u>What just happened?</u>

BONNIE. <u>Just wait, I'll explain.</u>

> (BONNIE *and* GREG *exit. Pause.*)

DONALD. You okay?

SHARON. Yeah, I'm –. I'm fine.

> (*Pause.* DONALD *leans into* SHARON.)

DONALD. You told Bonnie that it was an *accident?*

SHARON. No, I –! I just told her exactly what happened. I figured it was pretty clear that Zoe didn't lay down in the snow and freeze to death ten feet from her back door by *mistake.*

> (*Short pause.*)

DONALD. Should we tell her?

SHARON. No, just –. Let her believe what she wants, it doesn't matter.

> (DONALD *exits into the kitchen.*)
>
> (*After a moment,* SHARON *starts wrapping up some of the trinkets, putting them in boxes.*)
>
> (*A moment of silence. The TV plays.*)
>
> (*Then, from down the hall,* ZOE *enters.*)
>
> (*She enters carefully, looking around the room. She holds a cell phone in her hand. She goes closer to the TV, turning up the volume. We can now clearly hear the voice on the TV discussing products.* SHARON *continues packing items.*)

VOICE. – and it really is a wonderful value, it's a –, you know you really can just keep things like this for a very long time, it's something that will really last.

(ZOE *sits down, looking at the TV.*)

And it's really just about a wise investment, because at the end of the day this guy is gonna increase in value and end up being worth a lot more money than three easy installments of $29.99. And that's what makes this product so –

(ZOE *turns the volume back down to the lower level from before. She looks at the cell phone in her hand. Silence.*)

(ZOE *makes a call. She waits as the phone rings on the other end.*)

(*Finally:*)

ZOE. It's – me? Hi. You didn't pick up. Hi.

(*Pause.*)

I'm calling to –...

(*Pause.*)

I had this angel message last week? I was in a crosswalk, the corner of Main and 3rd, and I hear this message – "Dance, lovely, dance." That's all it was. And I had no idea what to think, I had no idea what to make of it, and then all of a sudden out of nowhere here comes this car, this *truck*, and it's blaring right through the stop sign and headed toward me. And all of the sudden, I knew what it meant, I knew what I had to do – I just turned really slowly, really elegantly, took a few steps. I just – danced with the truck. And I glide right alongside the edge of it as it speeds off and I'm in the middle of the intersection and people are asking me if I'm okay, and I –... "Dance, lovely, dance."

(*Pause.*)

ZOE. *(Cont.)* I just thought you'd like that, you used to love the angel messages I would get. I know you don't like me to talk about them anymore, but I thought you'd like that one. I thought you'd think it was funny, so maybe it was okay to tell you about that one. That's all.

>*(Pause. SHARON looks at ZOE.)*

Also, the uh –… The praying isn't working? And I know it's my fault, but I don't know what I'm doing wrong, and my temperature was over a hundred earlier, I'm feeling a little better now but it was over a hundred earlier, and I –…

>*(Pause.)*

I guess I was wondering if you could come? If you can, I know you're busy.

>*(Pause.)*

I love you very much, Sharon. My little healer.

>*(Short Pause.)*

Sorry, I know you don't like it when I –…

>*(Pause.)*

This message is really long sorry.

>*(Pause. ZOE looks at the phone, then ends the call.)*
>
>*(ZOE exits. SHARON watches her leave.)*
>
>*(The TV continues to play in the background.)*
>
>*(Then, finally, LAURA emerges from the hallway. She is still wearing her pajamas; she has her sleep mask in one hand. She takes a deep breath, turning off the overhead light.)*

SHARON. How's the migraine?

LAURA. Little better. I just can't sleep.

SHARON. I'm gonna start on the kitchen. You want anything, or –?

LAURA. I'm fine. You know where the remote is?

SHARON. You can change it on the TV.

LAURA. Eh.

>*(**LAURA** sits down, watching the TV.)*

>*(**SHARON** exits into the kitchen.)*

>*(After a moment, **GREG** enters, holding a trash bag. He sees **LAURA**.)*

GREG. Oh –

LAURA. It's fine. I couldn't sleep.

>*(Pause.)*

You're Greg, right? I'm Laura, I don't know if Bonnie told you about me. She said she was bringing someone, a new boyfriend. Nothing like taking a new lover to the funeral of someone your own age, huh?

>*(**GREG** indicates that he's deaf. **LAURA** realizes.)*

Oh shit sorry, I completely forgot, I –. Bonnie warned us, I should have –. I mean she didn't *warn* us, she just –. She just mentioned that you were deaf so we could – prepare, or –. Not that we *prepared*, I just…

>*(Pause.)*

I am – *really* glad that you can't hear what I'm saying right now.

GREG. I can read lips.

LAURA. Oh great.

>*(Awkward pause.)*

>*(Then, **GREG** smiles, offers her a hand. **LAURA** shakes his hand.)*

Yes, let's start over! I'm Laura.

GREG. Greg.

>*(They stand for a moment. Awkward pause.)*

LAURA. When I was a senior I did a sign version of "O Holy Night" for an assembly. Or rather, I was forced to do a sign version of "O Holy Night" for an assembly.

>*(**GREG** looks at her, confused.)*

You know, it's –. It's a Christmas carol?

> *(Short Pause.)*

It's like…

> **(LAURA** *starts singing/signing "O Holy Night."*
> *It's very awkward.)*

O Holy Night, the stars are brightly shining, it is the night of the dear Savior's birth.

> *(Short pause.* **LAURA** *tries to remember the sign for "fall".)*

Um. Oh.

> *(Resuming.)*

Fall on your knees! Oh, hear the angel's voices! O night divine –…

> **(LAURA** *stops, has no idea why she's doing this. An awkward silence.)*

> *(Finally,* **GREG** *smiles and claps politely.)*

Thank – you.

> **(LAURA** *sits down on the couch, rubbing her head. Pause.* **GREG** *goes to her.)*

GREG. You live in Montana?

LAURA. Yep, Montana. Missoula.

GREG. What do you do?

LAURA. I'm an associate professor at the University of Montana.

GREG. Wow.

> *(Pause.)*

LAURA. You're saying "wow" to associate professor at the University of Montana? You have a low "wow" threshold.

GREG. What do you teach?

LAURA. Baltic Studies?

> **(GREG** *looks at her, not understanding.)*

Baltic Studies? Baltic –? It's…

(GREG indicates that LAURA should write it down. LAURA finds something to write on and a pen. She writes it down, shows it to GREG.)

GREG. Oh!

LAURA. And – some comp lit, quarter time appointment in comp lit.

(GREG looks at her, not understanding. LAURA almost writes it down, then stops.)

Actually, it doesn't matter. It's mind-numbingly dull.

(Pause.)

GREG. Baltic Studies, that's –…

(Pause.)

I'm surprised the University of Montana has a Baltic Studies department.

LAURA. Well the University of Montana doesn't tend to think it has a Baltic Studies department, either. It's basically just me and a few adjuncts. What do you do?

GREG. Internet start-up.

LAURA. What kind?

(GREG pulls out his wallet, taking out a business card. He hands it to LAURA.)

"We manufacture and sell discount electric toothbrush heads over the internet directly to customers."

(Short pause.)

Catchy.

(Pause. LAURA hands the card back to GREG.)

How long have you and Bonnie been together?

GREG. Not long. Nine months.

LAURA. Nine months? That's long, that qualifies as long.

(LAURA continues to watch the TV. A few moments pass.)

(Then suddenly:)

GREG. Oh, Latvia!

> *(Pause.* LAURA *looks at him.)*

LAURA. Latvia?

GREG. Yeah, Latvia! That's where you're from, right?

> *(Pause.)*

LAURA. Yeah, I was born in Latvia, but I was seven when I was adopted, so I'm not really *from* there –

GREG. Bonnie says you speak Latvian?

LAURA. My Estonian is actually better than my Latvian, so it's really not –

GREG. That's really cool!

LAURA. *(Curt.)* But that's not why I got into Baltic Studies.

> *(Pause.)*

GREG. Oh.

LAURA. I mean it's not –… I just mean that I just happened to have an academic interest in the history and culture of the Baltic States.

> *(Awkward pause.* GREG *looks away.* LAURA *softens.)*

I don't really – talk very much about being from Latvia. So it's just – weird to be back with a bunch of people who know that about me. I'm not used to it.

> *(Pause.)*

GREG. Have you ever been back?

LAURA. To Latvia? Uh – yeah, I –. I went back once with the university.

> *(Pause.)*

I mean of course I still have some memories of being there, so maybe that –. I mean maybe that ignited my interest, but when I went there it really wasn't about that, it –…

> *(Pause.* GREG *looks at her.* LAURA *becomes more and more lost in thought.)*

There was actually this one moment during the trip, I –. I was with a professor from Riga, he was telling me all about this farm where you could get goat cheese that he said was the best in Europe, so we drove out of the city and into the countryside and I see these signs for a town called Remte which rings this very distant bell.

But it wasn't until we were actually driving through the town that we passed this big old concrete building, and I looked up to the second floor as we were driving past and I see this broken window – this window that's broken in this very specific way, this small triangle of glass missing with one vein of breakage going up to the opposite corner. And I realized – that building was the orphanage for disabled kids where I grew up. That broken window was *my* window. My entire life, that broken window has been just *sitting* there. How is that even possible? That broken window was from a different world, a different *reality* – a reality in which I only know a few words of English and my name is Ligita. But there it is, and now I'm speeding past it, and it's going to continue to just – be there, just be there, just…

(Pause. LAURA stops, looks at GREG.)

I'm really sorry, I shouldn't take Vicodin and interact with people.

(Short pause.)

Did you get any of that?

(Short pause.)

GREG. A little.

LAURA. I'm sorry, I –

(BONNIE enters, turning on the overhead lights.)

BONNIE. *(To GREG.)* There you are.

(Pause. BONNIE senses something.)

What?

LAURA. Nothing, sorry, I –. It's nothing.

GREG. <u>It's fine.</u>

(Short pause.)

BONNIE. *(To* **LAURA.** *)* How's the headache?

LAURA. Eh, still there.

BONNIE. Did you get any sleep?

LAURA. No, I –. No, I couldn't fall asleep.

BONNIE. Well, yeah, that makes sense.

(Pause.)

LAURA. What do you mean?

BONNIE. I mean sleeping in her *bed*, I couldn't sleep either.

LAURA. It's not that, I just couldn't –. Wait do you think it's weird that I'm staying here?

*(**BONNIE** starts packing up trinkets.)*

BONNIE. Whatever. If you're comfortable with it, then.

LAURA. I brought my own sheets.

BONNIE. Whatever! None of us cares! You know, the dust in the corners here is sort of out of control.

(To **GREG**, *simcom.)*

<u>Could you see if there's a vacuum in the hallway closet?</u>

*(**GREG** exits into the hallway.)*

LAURA. What do you mean "none of us"? Were you guys talking about it?

BONNIE. We just all said that if you're comfortable with it then fine. But I mean we all got hotel rooms, so.

LAURA. I *asked* you guys if you were comfortable with me staying here and you said *yes.*

BONNIE. And we are!

*(**GREG** re-enters with a dustbuster.)*

Oh great, that's better actually.

LAURA. I can get a hotel room if you guys are so uncomfortable with this.

BONNIE. Oh for Christ's sake, Laura, I said it's fine!

*(**BONNIE** turns on the dustbuster, cleaning the corners of the room. **GREG** starts packing up various items in the room.)*

LAURA. Well obviously it's not. I'm going to get my stuff together and find a hotel room –

BONNIE. It's after seven, on a Sunday! You'd have to drive all the way to Idaho Falls if you wanted to find a hotel room right now.

LAURA. Well if that's what I have to do, then I guess I'm heading to Idaho Falls.

BONNIE. Oh Jesus, will you just *stop*?

LAURA. Oh my God, Bonnie, turn off the fucking dust buster!

*(**BONNIE** turns off the dustbuster, stares at **LAURA**. A tense pause.)*

I'm sorry –

BONNIE. I have been through quite enough today, and I do *not* deserve you speaking to me in that tone.

(Pause.)

And I'm sorry, but you sleeping in her bed? It's strange, Laura. That's all I'm saying.

*(Pause. **LAURA** looks at **BONNIE** and **GREG**, relenting.)*

LAURA. You're right, I get it, I –. I'm sorry for shouting.

(Pause.)

And yes, I should have gotten a hotel, I just –. I don't know. This is all just – a lot to process.

(Pause.)

BONNIE. Okay.

LAURA. I mean I knew Zoe was unhappy, but I never thought she'd do *this*.

(Pause.)

BONNIE. What?

LAURA. When Sharon called, part of me wasn't surprised, but I guess…

>   *(Pause.)*

BONNIE. What are you…?

>   *(Pause.* **LAURA** *looks at* **BONNIE**.*)*

LAURA. Oh.

>   *(Short pause.)*

Oh… shit.

>   *(**BONNIE** exits toward the kitchen, **GREG** follows after her.)*
>
>   *(Pause.)*

Shit.

>   *(After a moment, **ZOE** enters from down the hall, weak, with a blanket wrapped around her shoulders. She heads toward the couch as **LAURA** exits back to the bedroom.)*
>
>   *(**ZOE** sits on the couch. She watches the TV. After a moment:)*

ZOE. *(Calling out.)* You find it okay?

SHARON. *(Offstage, calling from the kitchen.)* Yep.

>   *(Pause.)*

ZOE. *(Calling out.)* One Sweet'N Low.

SHARON. *(Offstage.)* Seriously?

ZOE. *(Calling out.)* What?

SHARON. *(Offstage.)* It's chemicals!

ZOE. *(Calling out.)* Oh, it's fine!

>   *(**ZOE** feels pain in her throat, swallows with some difficulty. **SHARON** comes out of the kitchen with a mug of tea for **ZOE**.)*

SHARON. I didn't give you Sweet'N Low, you shouldn't use Sweet'N Low.

ZOE. Why?

SHARON. I don't know, it's not healthy.

ZOE. Oh it's fine.

SHARON. Why is it that Sweet'N Low is okay but you won't take a pill every so often?

ZOE. Thank you.

> (SHARON *gives* ZOE *the mug,* ZOE *takes a sip.*)
>
> (ZOE *struggles to swallow, the effort hurting her throat.* SHARON *watches her.*)

I had to ask Tina for some days off.

SHARON. Was she okay about it?

ZOE. Oh you know her, she's –. I mean bless her but I swear that woman doesn't have any empathy at all. She told me I didn't have any sick days left, so.

SHARON. Wait, you don't have *any* sick days?

ZOE. I used some for a prayer retreat last spring, went to Denver for a week. Told Tina that I had the flu, that was wrong of me to do but I knew she wouldn't let me have the time off.

SHARON. So you –...? Are you gonna make rent this month?

> (*Pause.* ZOE *doesn't look at* SHARON.)

Do you – need some / help?

ZOE. I'm fine.

SHARON. I can / loan you some –

ZOE. I'm really fine, if I'm a couple weeks late it's not the end of the world, I –

SHARON. Zoe. Just let me help you out, okay?

> (*Pause.* ZOE *looks at* SHARON.)

ZOE. I'm so embarrassed.

SHARON. It's not a big deal, we've all been there.

ZOE. It's not just that, it's –. I call you out of the blue and you just drop everything and come out here, I feel like –. I don't know, I feel like a child sometimes. Like I can't take care of myself.

(**ZOE** *hears something on the TV.*)

ZOE. *(Cont.)* Oh are those the hands? I like those.

(**SHARON** *looks at the TV.*)

SHARON. A sculpture of severed hands?

ZOE. *Praying* hands. And they have the wood base, they're nice.

SHARON. It's creepy. Zoe, do *not* buy that –

ZOE. I'm *not* going to –. I'm not gonna buy it. I was just saying it's nice, that's all.

(*Pause.* **SHARON** *looks at the trinkets in the room.*)

SHARON. You've got – a *lot* of new little thingies.

ZOE. I –. I know it's silly, I'm not buying anything new. Sometimes I just get lonely, and it… I don't know, I just like knowing that even when I'm gone they'll still be around, and –. I just – like them. I know they're silly.

SHARON. I get it, I like ordering things too, you should see me with a couple glasses of wine and a laptop.

ZOE. No, it's not even that, it's –… I just like them, they're pretty, I like having them around. Knowing that they're here, that they'll always be here when I get home, and…

(*Pause.*)

I sound stupid.

SHARON. No, Zoe, you –. You don't.

(*Pause.*)

ZOE. *(Remembering.)* Oh, tell me about Tim!

SHARON. Zoe –

ZOE. I know you don't like it when I ask, but I don't care, I want to / hear about him.

SHARON. We've only been together for a few months, I don't know.

ZOE. Is he nice?

SHARON. He's fine.

ZOE. *He's not nice*?!

SHARON. He's nice! He's nice, geez.

ZOE. Where'd you meet?

SHARON. Online. I forget which. He's –…

(*Pause.*)

ZOE. What?

SHARON. It's embarrassing.

ZOE. What?!

(*Pause.*)

SHARON. He's a DJ.

ZOE. Like on the radio?

SHARON. Like weddings.

(*Pause.* ZOE *smiles a little.*)

Shut up.

ZOE. That's not anything to be embarrassed about!

SHARON. *Aggghhhh* and the annoying thing is he has this, like, *DJ voice* when he –… I mean in normal conversation he's *fine*, but then whenever he has a microphone it's like – he loses *all* self-awareness, it's horrifying. I need to break up with him.

ZOE. You can't break up with him because he's a wedding DJ!

SHARON. I think that is a *totally* legitimate reason to break up with someone.

ZOE. You're too picky.

SHARON. What does that even mean?

ZOE. It means you're too picky!

(*Pause.*)

Well anyway. You seem just fine on your own, who am I to give you advice?

(SHARON *smiles.* ZOE *takes a breath, takes the blanket off her shoulders.*)

Now I'm sweaty. Five minutes ago I was cold, now I'm sweaty. Father-Mother God, please let this be quick.

(*Pause.* SHARON *looks at her.*)

What?

SHARON. I don't think you have a cold.

(*Silence.*)

ZOE. When I called you I was just upset, I'm going to be fine, / I –

SHARON. The white stuff at the back of your throat? That's not a cold –

ZOE. I was just being a little crazy, I'm feeling better today.

SHARON. Your temperature is *higher* today, Zoe –

ZOE. So maybe you could just pray with me? Just a little?

(*Pause.* SHARON *looks away.*)

SHARON. I think you have strep throat, and it's not a big deal, but if you don't treat it and it gets worse, it could be a *very* big deal.

(*Pause.*)

There's an urgent care in Idaho Falls, I looked it up. You just need a prescription for a simple antibiotic, that's it.

(*Pause.*)

ZOE. Sharon.

SHARON. It's just – *so simple.* We can get a prescription called into the Walgreens on Fifth Street, we'll go together –

ZOE. No, Sharon –

SHARON. If it's strep throat, all you need is like a simple antibiotic! Antibiotics are *nothing*, they're like – mold or something! I think it's mold?

ZOE. It doesn't matter what –

SHARON. You don't even have to tell anyone!

ZOE. It's not about what I *tell* people, I –. Look I'm so grateful you're here, it was so sweet of you to come, but if you think you can just get me to go to a doctor, then you –

SHARON. *Please* just listen to me, Zoe –

ZOE. You can pray with me. That's what you can do.

(*Pause.*)

SHARON. No.

ZOE. You've done it before, Sharon. That summer at camp, I fell on the dock and hit my head?

SHARON. And you should have gone to the emergency room –

ZOE. But I didn't, and you prayed with me, and I was *healed.*

SHARON. You had a *concussion*, Zoe, and the only reason you didn't get seriously hurt was that we got lucky –

ZOE. I know you think you left this behind, but you have a gift, God gave you a gift of healing. And it was more than just the concussion. When my mom died? I was worried I'd never be happy again, but you prayed with me, every day, until that cloud lifted. And right now, if you really want to help me –

SHARON. I can't help you, okay?! I didn't heal you when we were kids, and I can't heal you now. Can you *try* to understand that?!

(*Short pause.*)

ZOE. You think I'm stupid.

SHARON. No –

ZOE. Yes, / you do –

SHARON. I don't think you're stupid, Zoe, I think you're a very smart person, actually. Which is why I don't understand why you can't just *grow up.*

(**ZOE** *looks at her. Pause.*)

I don't mean –. I didn't mean it to sound like –

ZOE. How old were you when you stopped believing? Thirteen?

(Pause.)

SHARON. Something like that.

ZOE. It was thirteen, I remember. Seventh grade, we were both in the seventh grade.

SHARON. Okay.

ZOE. And it *shook* me. I mean I always looked up to you, I still do. You were smart, independent, mature. So when you told me you had lost your faith, I felt like the world was disappearing underneath my feet. It wasn't until years later, I realized – you never even gave God a chance.

SHARON. I spent the majority of my *childhood* giving God a chance, Zoe –

ZOE. Childhood, exactly. You were a child. So now you think it's childish, you think that believing in a God is like believing in Santa or fairies. And I understand why you all got the camp shut down, I get it. Joan said some really misguided things to us, / she –

SHARON. "Misguided"? Zoe, she made us believe that there was something *spiritually* wrong with us –

ZOE. And that was awful, it was. But that doesn't mean that God doesn't exist!

SHARON. Zoe –

ZOE. And it wasn't easy for me, holding onto my faith. You have to face some pretty stark realities being a smart, religious person in your twenties, your thirties. You learn about suffering, injustice… And the easy thing to do is let go of the faith, submit to the idea that the world is dark and pointless, that's the *easy* out. The harder thing? Holding onto God, onto goodness. That's what I chose, and that's what I choose now. I choose a loving, truthful God over – *all* suffering, everywhere. My strep throat included.

(Pause. SHARON looks away.)

SHARON. Zoe, you –…

> (*Pause.*)

You could get *really, really* sick from this.

ZOE. So pray with me. Help me pray.

> (*Pause.*)

This isn't going to clear up on its own.

> (**SHARON** *looks at her, struggling. Silence.*)
>
> (*Finally,* **SHARON** *looks away. Pause.* **ZOE** *takes her mug and heads to the kitchen.*)

You want anything?

SHARON. No, I –.

> (*Short pause.*)

Zoe –

> (**ZOE** *exits to the kitchen without looking at* **SHARON**. **SHARON** *watches her go. Pause.*)
>
> (**BONNIE** *enters.*)

BONNIE. Hey.

SHARON. Hey.

BONNIE. What's going on?

> (*Pause.*)

SHARON. What do you – mean?

BONNIE. Laura said that –. She said that what happened to Zoe wasn't an accident.

> (*Pause.*)

SHARON. Oh.

> (*Pause.*)

BONNIE. *Why would she say that?!*

SHARON. I don't know, Bonnie! Ask her!

BONNIE. You don't have anything to say about this?!

SHARON. What do you want me to say?

BONNIE. Tell me that Laura's wrong! She's wrong, right?!

(LAURA enters from the bedroom, timid.)

LAURA. Uh – hey.

(Awkward pause. SHARON glares at LAURA.)

BONNIE. She didn't do that!

LAURA. / Yeah, of course.

SHARON. Yeah, she –. She didn't.

(Pause.)

BONNIE. She didn't!

LAURA. / Of course she didn't.

SHARON. No way.

(Another awkward silence.)

(Finally, DONALD enters, carrying a bizarre salt and pepper shaker set.)

DONALD. Does anybody know what the hell these are supposed to be? I feel like they're offensive to some group but I can't tell which.

(Pause. DONALD senses the tension.)

What's – up?

(Pause. GREG enters.)

LAURA. I just – I said something stupid about Zoe, and I was wrong, and I shouldn't have said it. That's all that it is.

(Short pause.)

DONALD. Oh.

(GREG goes to BONNIE.)

GREG. <u>You doing okay?</u>

BONNIE. *(Simcom.)* I don't know what's going on, they're not saying anything.

(Pause. GREG looks at BONNIE, hesitating.)

What?

GREG. <u>Don't you think it's a little weird that she froze to death outside? When you told me about it, I had my suspicions.</u>

BONNIE. <u>Why didn't you say anything?!</u>

GREG. <u>I didn't want you to get upset.</u>

BONNIE. *(Simcom.)* Well now I'm upset, Greg! Now I'm really upset, I…

> (**BONNIE** *takes a few breaths, calming down. Pause.)*

GREG. <u>Do you want an Ativan?</u>

BONNIE. <u>Yeah, thank you.</u>

> (**GREG** *exits to the kitchen. Silence.)*
>
> *(Finally:)*

If she…

> *(Short pause.)*

Why didn't she call one of us?

> *(Silence.* **BONNIE** *rummages around in her purse.* **GREG** *re-enters with water.)*

<u>I think I left them at the hotel.</u>

GREG. <u>Do you want me to get them?</u>

DONALD. *(To* **BONNIE**.*)* I have Xanax?

> *(Pause.)*

I mean if you want.

> *(Pause.)*

BONNIE. I take Ativan, actually. Xanax makes me dizzy.

DONALD. Gotcha.

BONNIE. <u>Yeah, please.</u>

GREG. I'll run to the hotel.

> (**GREG** *exits. Silence.)*
>
> *(Finally:)*

LAURA. Zoe actually – called me last week.

SHARON. Wait, she called you?

LAURA. Thursday, I think. Maybe Wednesday.

DONALD. Why didn't you say anything?

LAURA. Because she just –… I just don't want any of us reading too much into anything.

SHARON. What?

> *(Pause.)*

LAURA. We didn't talk very long, she said that she had just been thinking about me recently and wanted to know how I was doing.

DONALD. Did she seem – off?

LAURA. I mean she was always a little off, it was hard to tell, I –. It was mostly just small talk. But she did say she hadn't been feeling well.

DONALD. In what way?

LAURA. I don't know, I assumed – a cold, something. She said that she had been praying with people from the church to be healed, but that it wasn't working, and –.

> *(Pause.)*

She said – she was worried that the only person who could truly heal her was Sharon.

> *(Pause.)*

DONALD. She said –…? Wait, is this about – when Sharon would pray with her when we were kids, at the camp?

LAURA. I assumed, I don't know, / I –

SHARON. No, it's not that, she…

> *(**SHARON** trails off. Pause.)*

DONALD. What?

> *(Pause.)*

SHARON. Like three years ago, she got really sick. And when she described her symptoms to me on the phone, it sounded like strep throat. So I came to visit her, and tried to get her to go to the doctor, but she refused, and finally I –…

(Pause.)

I got a prescription for some antibiotics and started mixing it into her food for a week or so.

(Pause.)

And – she got better.

(Pause.)

DONALD. Oh.

*(Silence. **SHARON** looks away.)*

LAURA. But that doesn't mean –. There's still nothing you could have done –

SHARON. No, I –. I know.

(Pause.)

LAURA. Really.

SHARON. *I know,* I said.

(A very, very long silence. The TV drones.)

(Finally:)

LAURA. Okay.

(Pause.)

I'm going to try to say this in a way that doesn't make me sound like a terrible person. Because I'm not a terrible person, I'm really not. But I've thought a lot about this over the last few days, and I just…

(Pause.)

Zoe and I were very different people, but the one thing we always had in common is that we were both – *so* unhappy. Even when we were kids. And we dealt with it in very different ways. I deal with it by going to therapy and taking antidepressants. And that doesn't make me a *happy* person necessarily, it just – lifts me up enough so I can go to work and have relationships with other people. But Zoe dealt with it in a drastically different way, in a way that actually made her – happy. She dealt with it by desperately believing that the material world was an illusion and that she could pray away the flu. But I also think, for an intelligent person like Zoe? There would be a moment where she couldn't persuade herself to believe in all that anymore. And if she deliberately laid herself down in the snow out there, it was probably because she could feel that moment coming.

(Short pause.)

LAURA. *(Cont.)* So maybe this is just – her choice. Maybe it's not a huge tragedy, maybe we just need to – respect her decision.

(Pause.)

That's what I think.

(Silence.)

BONNIE. *(To LAURA, simply.)* You are a terrible person.

LAURA. Okay. I'm done now.

(Short pause.)

Goodnight, everyone.

(LAURA exits into the bedroom.)

(A long silence. Finally, SHARON heads for the kitchen.)

SHARON. I found an aide in Pocatello, she should be here in a couple hours. I'm just gonna work on the kitchen until then.

DONALD. Sharon –

(SHARON exits.)

(The TV drones. BONNIE stares forward. Silence.)

(Finally:)

I'm sorry we didn't just tell you –

BONNIE. It's fine, I –.

(Pause.)

I know it's obvious. Maybe I just didn't want to believe it.

(Pause.)

Is Sharon okay?

DONALD. I'd just – give her a minute.

*(Short pause. **BONNIE** heads for some items in the room.)*

BONNIE. Are these throw-away, or –?

DONALD. Those are all donate, I think.

(Short pause.)

Are you sure you don't wanna call it a night, head back to the hotel?

BONNIE. Nah, I wouldn't be able to sleep, anyway.

*(**BONNIE** and **DONALD** resume packing. Silence.)*

I think it's also just – I'm not used to having someone my own age die?

DONALD. Yeah, totally. It's – crazy.

BONNIE. I mean that'll change eventually, but right now it just – doesn't even feel real.

DONALD. Yeah.

(They pack for a few more moments.)

Like a year ago, I got a phone call from my mom and she said that my cousin Barry had cancer. I forget which kind, but really aggressive. And Barry was like two years *younger* than me. He lived in Oregon, I hadn't seen him since I was like fourteen years old, we never really had a relationship. But I felt so paralyzed, I didn't know what I was supposed to do in that situation. Like, should I call him, visit him? But really, does this man who only has a few months left to live really need to talk with this guy he barely knows who just happens to be his cousin? But then you start wondering if that's just a way to justify not getting in touch. A way to justify not having to interact with a dying person.

(Pause.)

DONALD. *(Cont.)* So I didn't do anything. And then like two or three months later, my mom calls me back and says that Barry died last night. And then she says that Barry had *asked* about me. Like, a day or so before he died, he had asked how I was doing.

(Long pause.)

I really wonder sometimes if I'm not a good person.

(Pause.)

BONNIE. Jesus, Donald, you really need a boyfriend.

DONALD. That's not –. That won't, like, *fix* anything.

BONNIE. It'll help! You need someone in your life to convince you that you're not a bad person!

DONALD. I mean, I don't think I'm a bad person. Well, I mean I'm pretty sure I'm not a *very* bad person. I don't like – torture children. God, why did I go there right off the bat?

BONNIE. You know I was in pretty bad shape last year, and Greg really helped get me out of it.

(DONALD turns to her.)

DONALD. What was going on?

BONNIE. Panic attacks. Couple that sent me to the hospital they were so bad.

DONALD. Oh, wow.

BONNIE. And of course the worst thing about it was – things were *fine.* I was healthy, money was okay, everything at the office was fine. Which just made me angry at myself for not feeling normal. Anyway, one day I ended up having an attack at work, and one of the other dental hygienists decided it would be good for me to get out there, meet people – and she ended up setting me up with Greg. We had our first date the next night.

DONALD. Oh, that's so sweet.

BONNIE. No, it wasn't, it was a disaster. After I said yes, I realized that the only reason she set us up was because he's deaf, as if that means we have something in *common*, or –. So I basically sabotaged the date, I chose this cheesy Italian restaurant out by the mall, wore this, like, *really* unflattering T-shirt. But then I get there, and I see Greg, and I was like – woah.

DONALD. Yeah, he's –. Yeah.

BONNIE. Right?! And then we get like five minutes into the date, and I realize that not only is he that good looking but he's also *nice* which is just insane. So then I just start – freaking out, and I'm so worked up I don't notice that I've had two martinis in less than twenty minutes. So then I'm *drunk*.

DONALD. Eesh.

BONNIE. Yeah. And what do I do? I look him straight in the eye and I say, "I'm sorry, I got a little drunk because you being deaf makes me nervous, so I'm not gonna be able to talk for at least twenty minutes." I *actually* said that.

DONALD. Oh, God.

BONNIE. *I know.* But then – he looked at me and he said – "No worries." And he sat there patiently for twenty minutes, while I ate an entire basket of bread. Turns out he actually *liked* that I had said that, he told me that he had gone on all these dates with women who were walking on eggshells the entire time, and he loved that I just – say what I think.

(*Pause.*)

I was like – who is this man? Who is this person who can just live their life moment to moment like that, who can just – be nice and open and… And I thought, maybe if I'm with this person, maybe I can be like that someday. Maybe it'll rub off somehow. Maybe it'll – help.

(*Pause.*)

DONALD. Has it?

(**BONNIE** *pauses, stops packing.* **DONALD** *stops packing as well, watching her.*)

(A long silence.)

DONALD. *(Cont.)* You – okay?

(Pause.)

BONNIE. Yeah so anyway I just understand how Zoe must've felt.

(Pause.)

DONALD. I don't think that was the point you were making, Bonnie.

BONNIE. Hm?

DONALD. You were trying to tell me that a boyfriend could make me feel better. That's why you told me all that.

BONNIE. Yeah well that too.

(Pause. BONNIE moves toward the front door.)

I'm going to have a cigarette, do you want a cigarette?

DONALD. Oh, I don't smoke.

(Pause.)

What kind are they?

BONNIE. Parliaments.

DONALD. Yeah, okay.

(BONNIE and DONALD head out the front door.)

(As they exit, ZOE enters, holding the copy of Science and Health with a Key to the Scriptures. *She sits down on the couch, reading it.)*

(SHARON enters from the kitchen. She looks at ZOE. ZOE looks up at SHARON. Pause.)

(ZOE puts away the book, looks away.)

(Silence.)

(SHARON approaches ZOE. She closes her eyes, bows her head.)

SHARON. Father-Mother God.

(ZOE smiles, closing her eyes as well.)

We ask you that –... We ask you to – come to this woman.
We ask you to come to this woman and – relieve her of
her – suffering? We ask –...

> (*Pause.* **SHARON** *opens her eyes, looking at* **ZOE**.)

> (**ZOE** *opens her eyes as well.*)

ZOE. What?

> (*Pause.*)

SHARON. Zoe, why do you have strep throat?

> (*Pause.*)

ZOE. I don't know.

SHARON. Sickness is a spiritual issue, right?

> (*Pause.*)

So why do you have a sore throat?

> (*Pause.*)

ZOE. I don't feel good.

SHARON. Why don't you feel good?

ZOE. Sharon, please just pray with me –

SHARON. I am. Why don't you feel good?

> (*Pause.*)

ZOE. I don't know what –. I don't know what I'm doing.

SHARON. With what?

ZOE. I don't know, with anything, with...

> (*Pause.*)

I get up in the morning, I make the same breakfast
every day. I look outside and I try to tell myself I should
feel good about going to work. I should feel good about
living a life, I should feel grateful. Then I –...

SHARON. What?

ZOE. I'm just – *unhappy.*

SHARON. Why?

ZOE. Because nothing matters. Nothing I do matters. My
little job, my little life, nothing is going to *last*, it all

just ends, and when I leave the world's gonna be the same, nothing will be different, and I think about that *all day long*. I think about it at work, I think about it when I come home, I think about it when I go to bed, and it –…

> *(Pause.)*

SHARON. What?

ZOE. I'm asking for God and I'm not getting anything.

> *(Pause.)*

I'm worried that God isn't in my life anymore.

> *(Pause.)*

I'm worried that God doesn't –…

> *(Silence. **SHARON** watches **ZOE** as she breathes in and out, increasingly upset.)*
>
> *(Finally:)*

SHARON. God is watching over you, Zoe. God loves you, and is watching over you.

> *(Pause.)*

Just – try to take comfort in that, okay? I promise you that God is watching over you, and that he's going to cure this. He's going to make this better.

> *(Pause.)*

I swear.

> *(Another silence. **ZOE** looks at **SHARON**, then smiles.)*

ZOE. Amen.

> *(Silence. **ZOE** takes a few deep breaths.)*

SHARON. Are you –? You okay?

ZOE. Yes. Yes, I am.

> *(Pause.)*

I love you very much.

> *(Pause. **ZOE** smiles at her.)*

SHARON. You should sleep.

> (*Pause.* ZOE *takes a breath, then gets up, exiting into her bedroom.* SHARON *watches her go.*)

> (SHARON *is left with the book in her hands. She looks at it.*)

> (*After a moment,* DONALD *re-enters. He sees* SHARON *with the book.* SHARON *looks at him.*)

DONALD. Hey.

> (*Silence.*)

You okay?

> (*Pause.*)

SHARON. She could have made this easier, you know?

DONALD. What?

SHARON. If Zoe knew she was going to –, it's so *selfish*. She gets to just abandon ship and we're the ones who get to clean up her *fucking mess*, she –.

> (*Pause.*)

I just don't know why she couldn't have left all this religious shit behind when we did, you know?

> (*Pause.*)

DONALD. I don't know if you can just *blame* her church for this –

SHARON. Why not? She still went to that church every Sunday, she probably saw Joan there all the time –

DONALD. But for all you know that was a good thing for her.

> (*Pause.* SHARON *looks at* DONALD.)

SHARON. You think Zoe believing that she could pray away strep throat is a "good" thing?

DONALD. I'm just saying that we'll never know why she did this, so there's no / use –!

SHARON. I knew her better than you, Donald, I'm the / one who –

DONALD. Wait, what?

(*Short pause.*)

SHARON. Nevermind.

DONALD. She was my friend too, Sharon.

SHARON. I know.

DONALD. You're not the only one who lost someone this week.

SHARON. But I am the one who showed up the day after it happened. I'm the one who paid for the funeral, I'm the one / who –

DONALD. Is that what this is about? I'll pay you back when I can, I told you –

> (**BONNIE** *and* **GREG** *enter from outside. Throughout the following,* **BONNIE** *interprets for* **GREG** *as best as she can.*)

SHARON. Nevermind! Just forget it.

DONALD. Sharon, where is this coming from?!

SHARON. I said forget it!

GREG. (*To* **BONNIE**.) <u>What's going on?</u>

BONNIE. Guys – what's going on?

DONALD. Sharon is pissed that we didn't chip in for the funeral.

BONNIE. <u>/ Something about money for the funeral?</u>

SHARON. Oh my God, Donald, I didn't say that!

> (**LAURA** *enters.*)

LAURA. Okay, what the fuck.

GREG. <u>/ They're arguing about money?</u>

DONALD. Well I don't know why else you're freaking out on me like this –

BONNIE. <u>/ I guess? I don't know.</u>

SHARON. Zoe didn't ask for help when she needed it because she thought that her depression was a *spiritual* problem. And then you show up here and you invite *Joan* to the funeral?! How could you do that?!

*(*BONNIE, LAURA, *and* GREG *look at* DONALD.*)*

LAURA. You invited Joan?

BONNIE. / Donald invited Joan to the funeral.

DONALD. I'm sorry, Sharon, I already said that I was sorry, I was just trying to be a decent / human being –

SHARON. And now you're gonna look me in the eye and tell me that her believing in all that crap was a *good* thing?!

BONNIE. / They're arguing about Zoe and religion…

DONALD. I didn't say that! All I said is that *faith* is a good thing, that maybe it was a comfort to her, maybe it –!

(Short pause.)

And actually, if you really want to know the truth, I go to a church! It's a Unitarian church, the pastor is a lesbian named Karen, and she's *wonderful!*

BONNIE. / Donald goes to church.

SHARON. You go to a *church?*

GREG. / Why is that such a big deal? You go to a church.

DONALD. Okay, don't –. Not everyone lives so happily in cold stark atheism, Sharon, some people like to *believe* in something.

BONNIE. / Yeah, but I wouldn't tell Sharon.

SHARON. So – I don't *believe* in anything?

GREG. / Why?

DONALD. I didn't say that, I just…

(Pause. DONALD *collects himself.)*

BONNIE. / It's complicated… You know, the camp.

DONALD. I'm just saying – Joan said some terrible things to us, she was awful. But I don't think that has anything to do with the fact that I go to a church. That's all I'm saying.

(Silence.)

LAURA. I have a church I go to sometimes.

(Short pause.)

BONNIE. / <u>Laura goes to church, too.</u>

LAURA. It's nice. It's Episcopalian. Sometimes it's nice to just go and see people. They give you coffee and cookies after.

(*Pause.* **BONNIE** *looks at* **GREG**.)

GREG. <u>Go ahead.</u>

(*Pause.* **BONNIE** *looks at* **SHARON**.)

BONNIE. … Lutheran.

(*Silence.* **SHARON** *looks around the room.*)

SHARON. Huh.

(*Pause.*)

I guess I just thought – you were all more intelligent than this.

(*Pause.* **SHARON** *takes out her phone.*)

My aide should be here in a couple hours, I'm just gonna work on the kitchen until then.

DONALD. Sharon, let's just please talk about this tomorrow.

SHARON. No, I actually think I'm gonna take off tomorrow.

(**SHARON** *takes out her phone, looking at it.*)

DONALD. Please, / you don't have to –

BONNIE. / <u>Sharon's leaving tomorrow.</u>

LAURA. / Sharon, c'mon –

SHARON. I really shouldn't be taking this much time off work, anyway, and it's gonna be expensive to bring aides out here, and –. If you guys need help packing stuff up I can hire someone.

(*Pause.*)

Okay?

(**SHARON** *looks at them. Pause.*)

LAURA. Okay.

(**SHARON** *exits into the kitchen.*)

DONALD. Look, let's just – all go get some sleep, okay?

LAURA. Yeah, okay.

(Pause. Finally, **GREG** *faces the group.)*

GREG. <u>Why did you guys keep going back every summer?</u>

BONNIE. He's asking why we kept going back to the camp every summer.

LAURA. I mean – our parents would send us there.

GREG. **But you could have told your parents you hated it, you didn't have to go.**

DONALD. I mean, yeah, I guess we didn't *have* to go –

GREG. **I'm just wondering if there were any good things about it apart from the Scientology stuff.**

LAURA. Christian Science.

GREG. Whatever. **I went to a deaf camp when I was a kid one summer, I hated it. I refused to go back the next year. And no one at that camp was telling me that I could pray myself into a hearing person. I just hated the food and the bugs and I wasn't one of the popular kids.**

DONALD. I mean, I guess we just didn't know any better? We just got used to hearing all that stuff.

LAURA. Are you wondering *why* we got it shut down, or –?

GREG. **No, no, I understand why you got it shut down, I understand Joan was terrible. But were there any good things about it?**

(Pause.)

LAURA. I guess – the good parts don't really stick with you like the bad parts do.

(Pause.)

GREG. Huh.

(Pause.)

I'll get the car.

(**GREG** *exits. A silence apart from the TV droning in the background.* **DONALD**, **BONNIE**, *and* **LAURA**'s *gazes all drift toward the TV.*)

DONALD. Yeah, I mean –... I guess I must have had – fun. Right?

(*Pause.*)

BONNIE. I'm assuming we did. I kept going until I was twelve.

DONALD. I was thirteen.

(*Pause.*)

LAURA. Huh. Yeah, I –. I don't know.

(**GREG** *re-enters.*)

GREG. Bonnie.

BONNIE. Yeah?

(**GREG** *looks toward the doorway.*)

(*Then, from behind* **GREG**, **JOAN** *enters.*)

(**LAURA**, **BONNIE**, *and* **DONALD** *all look up, seeing* **JOAN**. *A tense pause.*)

JOAN. Hi kids.

(*Silence.*)

I hope –...

(*Pause.*)

I hope this is okay?

(*Then,* **SHARON** *re-enters with her phone in her hand. She sees* **JOAN**, *stops.*)

(*Tense pause.* **GREG** *faces everyone.*)

GREG. I can wait in the kitchen.

(**GREG** *exits to the kitchen.* **DONALD** *goes to the TV, turning it off.*)

(*Awkward silence.*)

JOAN. I'll make this quick. It's just that I saw you all at the funeral, and –. Amazing, seeing you all after all this time, you –. Anyway – I just wanted to give you this.

> (JOAN *pulls out an old, small plastic frog.*)

> (LAURA, BONNIE, SHARON, *and* DONALD *immediately recognize it.*)

You all remember it?

> (*Pause.*)

DONALD. Yeah, we –. Yeah.

JOAN. Last summer, I was clearing some old overgrowth near the pond, I looked down and there it was. It's been sitting there for over twenty-five years. I recognized it immediately, I don't remember ever seeing Zoe without it most summers. I still don't know why she was so attached to it. That summer when she was nine or ten, when she lost it, I couldn't understand why she was so upset.

> (*Pause.*)

Anyway, I don't know if it helps any of you, but when I found this little frog – I suddenly remembered how happy Zoe was, once. And that was comforting.

> (*Pause.*)

I just – thought you all should have it.

> (JOAN *puts the frog down on the couch. A tense pause.*)

> (GREG *exits to the kitchen.* JOAN *moves to exit.*)

I can – I can leave you kids alone, I don't have to –

SHARON. That's it?

> (*Pause.* JOAN *looks at* SHARON.)

After all this time, you don't have anything to say to us?

> (*Pause.*)

JOAN. I just – didn't want to presume that any of you wanted me to…

(Pause.)

After everything with the camp, shutting it down… You all have to realize, until that article came out in the *Post Register*, until I read those quotes from you all about what I had said – I was fairly oblivious to what I was really doing. Honestly, it's still hard for me to understand how I could have done so much harm to you all when I was so certain that there was nothing but love in my heart.

SHARON. You told me I could pray myself out of this wheelchair, Joan.

(Pause.)

JOAN. My God, I did say that, didn't I?

(Pause.)

There's no way I can defend any of the things I said to you kids back then. And if I could take it back, I would, but I –

SHARON. You're not actually sorry, are you?

(Pause.)

JOAN. Sharon –

SHARON. For telling us all those things when we were kids, for filling Zoe's head up with all that stuff.

JOAN. If I had any idea that things had gotten this bad for Zoe, I promise / I –

SHARON. The only reason she was into Christian Science in the first place was because of you. And now you –

JOAN. Sharon, I told her years ago that she should consider leaving the church. Like I did.

*(Pause. Everyone looks at **JOAN**.)*

DONALD. Wait, you –?

JOAN. We didn't have it out or anything, but around the time I left the church, I could tell that things were getting – strange for her. She'd always talk about these angel messages she was getting, at first I didn't think much of them until I visited here one day and saw that the fridge was empty because she had received an angel message that day before telling her to get rid of all her food.

LAURA. So why didn't you do anything?

JOAN. I tried to. I begged her to find a therapist, to find some help, but she –

DONALD. You could have called one of us.

JOAN. I figured none of you would enjoy hearing from me all that much. Though I should have contacted one of you, I should have.

(Pause.)

I promise you that I felt nothing but love for you all, and for Zoe. And I do think that – for what it's worth – Zoe took a lot of joy in her faith –

SHARON. There it is. You're not even sorry.

(Pause.)

JOAN. Sharon, when you were nine or so, I think it was either the second or third summer you came to camp – you had those constant nightmares, you remember those?

SHARON. Okay, I know what you're doing –

JOAN. And I had that little cross, that little plastic cross and I told you to sleep with it under your pillow and you told me that the nightmares had / stopped –

SHARON. They didn't stop because of a cross –

JOAN. Of course they didn't! It was a plastic cross that broke off of a cheap nativity scene that I bought in the late seventies! But it compelled something in you, it *helped* you –

SHARON. Zoe didn't kill herself because of *nightmares*, Zoe was suffering and you made her believe that it was a *spiritual* problem –

JOAN. Alright, obviously I / shouldn't have come here –

DONALD. Okay, let's just calm / down –

LAURA. / Sharon –

JOAN. And I'm sorry that I said those things to you, I'm sorry I couldn't help Zoe –

SHARON. Word garbage.

JOAN. I don't know what you want me to say!

SHARON. I want you to say it's your fault that Zoe's dead!

(Silence.)

(Finally:)

JOAN. I can't.

SHARON. Why?

JOAN. Because I don't know if I could live my life at all if I believed that. I have to believe that I did her *some* good.

(Pause.)

SHARON. Well. There it is.

JOAN. Yes.

(Pause. **SHARON** *turns away from* **JOAN.** **JOAN** *prepares to leave.)*

There's just –.

(Pause.)

I'd just like to go in her room, just for a moment. I'd just like to see it before it gets taken apart, I'd like to remember her just for a minute. If that's okay with you all.

*(***SHARON*** *doesn't look at* **JOAN.** *Pause.)*

LAURA. Yeah, that's fine.

JOAN. Thank you.

*(***JOAN*** *makes her way into* **ZOE**'s *bedroom. Silence.)*

LAURA. I think I'm gonna head to Idaho Falls, see if I can find a hotel for the night.

BONNIE. Laura, you don't have to –

LAURA. No, it's really not you. You're right, I should have done this in the first place.

(LAURA turns toward the hallway.)

BONNIE. *(To LAURA.)* You know we have an extra bed in our hotel room? You could just ride with us.

> *(Pause.)*

If you want privacy, I get it, I just –

LAURA. No, that –. That sounds nice. Thanks.

BONNIE. I'm gonna get Greg.

> *(LAURA exits down the hall. BONNIE goes into the kitchen to get GREG.)*
>
> *(DONALD sits down.)*

DONALD. Alright, Sharon, let's –. Joan'll be gone soon, let's just –.

> *(Pause.)*

Sharon?

> *(Pause. SHARON doesn't respond, lost in thought.)*

Look, I'm sorry for –. What I said earlier, I –.

> *(Short pause.)*

I just think – what Zoe did was a lot more complicated than something that Christian Science did to her. And it was a lot more complicated than you slipping some pills into her food.

SHARON. Are you sure?

> *(Pause.)*
>
> *(BONNIE and GREG re-enter.)*

BONNIE. We'll be back in the morning to pack.

> *(Short pause.)*

Sharon, are you – leaving tomorrow?

> *(Pause. SHARON looks down, not responding. LAURA re-enters wearing a coat and shoes, holding a suitcase.)*

If you do leave – thank you for putting the funeral together. It means a lot.

(**BONNIE**, **GREG**, *and* **LAURA** *leave.*)

(**DONALD** *and* **SHARON** *are left alone.*)

(*Silence.*)

SHARON. I don't understand why I can't get past this.

(*Pause.*)

Why can't I just get past this?

(*Pause.*)

DONALD. You just need to – forget about her, she's just some sad lady living alone in a tiny little town. You got the camp shut down, she doesn't even believe in that stuff anymore, you *won*. Right?

(*Pause.*)

(**JOAN** *re-enters. She pauses for a moment.*)

Bonnie and Laura took off.

JOAN. Yes, she –. Laura told me.

(*Pause.*)

It was – nice seeing you kids again.

(*Pause.* **JOAN** *heads for the exit.*)

SHARON. Wait.

(**JOAN** *stops. Silence.*)

Donald, could you head back to the hotel?

(*Pause.*)

DONALD. You sure?

SHARON. Yeah.

DONALD. I can just wait in the bedroom –

SHARON. It's fine, really, I'll call you later, just –.

(*Pause.*)

DONALD. Yeah, okay.

SHARON. Thanks.

(*Pause.* **DONALD** *looks at* **JOAN**, *then exits.*)

(JOAN, *unsure of what to do, stays standing near the door. Pause.*)

Its name was Cabinet.

(*Pause.*)

That frog. Zoe had named it Cabinet.

(*Pause.* JOAN *looks at* SHARON.)

JOAN. She did?

SHARON. Yeah.

JOAN. I didn't know that. That seems like something I'd remember, I'm surprised.

(*Short pause.*)

I remember one summer – when we did that trip to Twin Falls to see the play, was that it?

SHARON. I'm not sure…

JOAN. I don't even remember what the play was, in my mind it was *A Christmas Carol*, but that doesn't make any sense. Gosh, what was it?

SHARON. Are you sure it was a play? I remember seeing ballet one time –?

JOAN. Though wasn't that the Boise trip?

SHARON. I thought Boise was the state history museum trip.

JOAN. Well it was but –… Oh, I don't know. Anyway, Zoe left it there, didn't realize until we were all back at the camp. She was so upset, for some reason it meant so much to her. So I had to drive all the way back to that theater to get it.

(*Pause.*)

When I found it outside last summer, I thought about calling Zoe, but I figured she didn't want to hear from me. I should have tried, at least.

(*Silence.*)

SHARON. So you – really don't believe in any of that stuff anymore?

(Pause.)

JOAN. Well, that's –. That's the question, I guess. I'm not sure if I've entirely let go of my faith, but I've – made room for other things? Something like that?

(Pause.)

It wasn't easy, trying to find meaning in worldly things for the first time. Volunteer here and there, read books, listen to Bach, maybe write a poem or two I'd never show anyone. And – go to the doctor. Take a pill now and then. But – I don't think Zoe was capable of making that shift. To take herself out of the spiritual realm and live down here, with the rest of us.

(Pause.)

But I'm glad that you were still in touch with her, that's comforting to know. I'm sure you did her a lot of good.

(Silence.)

SHARON. I want to believe that. I want to believe I helped her while she was alive, I want to believe that there wasn't anything I could have done, but –…

(Silence.)

JOAN. There are just some people who have a hard time with – not knowing why. People like Zoe.

(Pause.)

SHARON. And us.

JOAN. I'm working on it.

(Short pause.)

I'm working on it.

(Silence. JOAN and SHARON breathe.)

(Finally:)

Where are you staying?

(Pause.)

SHARON. I have a room at the Best Western.

JOAN. Oh.

> *(Pause.)*

They have a hot tub.

SHARON. Yep.

JOAN. Don't go in it, though, I've heard –. It's disgusting, I won't tell you the story. Just don't go in.

> *(Pause.)*

You – don't have an aide with you?

SHARON. Oh, I –. She had to go back to Chicago. I had another guy who was gonna come in, but I actually got a text a little bit ago, he can't make it.

JOAN. I might be able to – I used to know someone in Idaho Falls –

SHARON. No, it's –. It's okay. I found someone in Austin who can come in tomorrow, be with me for a few days while we finish packing up. I'll text Donald, he can come pick me up, help me out for the night.

> *(**SHARON** pulls out her phone, sends a quick text.)*

> *(**JOAN** feels something in the couch under her seat. She reaches into the cushion, pulling out the remote control. **SHARON** sees it.)*

Huh.

> *(**JOAN** turns on the TV.)*

JOAN. Shopping channel.

SHARON. That's fine.

> *(Silence. They watch for a moment.)*

We've only got two days to pack up the whole house. Landlord is gonna replace the carpets, repaint all the walls.

JOAN. That's fast.

SHARON. Yeah.

> *(Pause.)*

The last funeral I was at was like five years ago. My grandma. I had this weird moment where I realized – my grandma had a grandma, too. My great-great-grandma. But I don't know anything about her. I don't know her name, what she looked like, how she died. She's just – gone. And the last person who might have remembered anything about her just died.

(Pause.)

But then I realized that there are certain things, like – things she said to her grandkids, or did to her grandkids. Both good things and bad things. And then those grandkids said or did those things to their own grandkids without even realizing. So there's like – something there. Something goes on.

(Pause.)

I don't know, maybe that's dumb.

JOAN. No, I –.

(Pause.)

I think that's right.

(Blackout.)

End of Play